Benny Dubious Playbook Scheme Trouble in Georgia Book 2: "Moshie's" Fall

Benny Dubious Playbook Scheme Series 3, Volume 2

Maxwell Hoffman

Published by Maxwell Hoffman, 2024.

This is a work of fiction. Similarities to real people, places, or events are entirely coincidental.

BENNY DUBIOUS PLAYBOOK SCHEME TROUBLE IN GEORGIA BOOK 2: "MOSHIE'S" FALL

First edition. October 17, 2024.

Copyright © 2024 Maxwell Hoffman.

ISBN: 979-8227281586

Written by Maxwell Hoffman.

Also by Maxwell Hoffman

Benny Dubious Playbook Scheme Series 3
Benny Dubious Playbook Scheme Trouble in Georgia: The Moshie Affair
Benny Dubious Playbook Scheme Trouble in Georgia Book 2: "Moshie's" Fall

Misadventures of Wolfgang Wirrarr
Misadventures of Wolfgang Wirrarr Omnibus Trilogy

Rowan Sunfire Frosty Fugitive Series
Rowan Sunfire Frosty Fugitive Book 3 Defense of Vos Tower
Rowan Sunfire Frosty Fugitive Omnibus Trilogy

Watch for more at https://www.instagram.com/vader7800/.

Table of Contents

Benny Dubious Playbook Scheme Trouble in Georgia Book 2: "Moshie's" Fall (Benny Dubious Playbook Scheme Series 3, #2)............1

Part One 3

Prologue..5

Chapter One..13

Chapter Two..21

Chapter Three 29

Part Two 37

Chapter Four 39

Chapter Five 49

Chapter Six 59

Chapter Seven 67

Part Three..75

Chapter Eight..77

Chapter Nine...85

Chapter Ten 93

Epilogue... 101

BENNY DUBIOUS PLAYBOOK SCHEME
TROUBLE IN GEORGIA BOOK 2
"MOSHIE'S" FALL
by
Maxwell Hoffman

Part One

Prologue

<u>Picking Up Nia</u>

#

Hugo Roth under his persona "Moshie Scheinman" soon arrived at Ms. Nia Hope Carver's apartment. She had her usual lawyer-like suit on as she emerged. She could see her new boyfriend pulling up to the parking lot.

#

"I will be right there" said Nia.

#

Nia soon headed downstairs and towards the parking lot and got into the shotgun seat. She soon sent her campaign manager - Ashura Clark a text message.

#

"I will be arriving at my campaign event shortly with my boyfriend" said Nia.

#

Ashura on the other end rolled her eyes, she could get the feeling that something was off with this "Moshie". That this Jewish rapper rose to fame overnight just by dating Nia. Ashura couldn't explain it, but she felt that former President Harold Truax had something to do with all of this.

#

"Feeling uneasy?" asked Senator Amos.

#

Senator Amos Carver III knew the campaign manager had a similar view of "Moshie" as he did. He could tell that there was something odd and off about his demeanor altogether.

#

"I don't feel right about this Moshie" said Ashura.

#

"I don't blame you" said Senator Amos, "but we have to make due with what we have until we have further information."

#

As Hugo drove off with Nia, Hugo was unaware he was being followed by Agent GA in an unmarked police car.

#

<u>Tagging Along</u>

#

Since Benny Dubious was already spotted by the Blue Eagle Collective spies, Benny wasn't anywhere near the event. This operation was all going to be relied upon by Hugo Roth. Hugo had butterflies in him as he continued to drive towards the event, this event was a sports event, particularly a soccer match. Once Hugo parked his car in the parking lot, both he and Nia soon headed towards the arena.

#

"There's his car" said Agent GA as he soon arrived.

#

Agent GA soon wrote down the license plate information on the car itself. What a fool, that if this wasn't "Moshie Scheinman" he would figure out who was the owner of the car.

#

"Let's send this to the boys and girls back in the IT area" said Agent GA to himself.

#

The Blue Eagle Collective agent soon sent the license plate, back in the IT division of the Blue Eagle Collective, the IT personal gazed at the license plate.

#

"Georgia license plate, we will do a check on it and report our findings within a day" said the IT personal on the other end.

#

"Splendid" said Agent GA in a reply email.

#

The agent was pleased that he did most of the work, he would have high hopes it would be linked back to Samuel Roth.

#

<u>The Soccer Game</u>

#

Hugo didn't seem to care that much about sports, he was just into being with Nia even under his "Moshie" persona. The two sat down near Senator Amos who already had seats for them.

#

"Glad you could make it" said Senator Amos, "there are so many people here all because of you."

#

On the big screen for the soccer match, Nia and Hugo's faces soon appeared which the audience from both sides of the match soon cheered. It was much to Ashura's disgust that she felt "Moshie" was a distraction from Nia's campaign duties.

#

"This is a distraction to your daughter's campaign duties" whispered Ashura.

#

Ashura didn't want to alarm Nia, at least not just yet. But she felt she had to let her father know.

#

"I am aware of it" whispered Senator Amos, "we just have to play along with this."

#

On the other end of the soccer stadium sat Samuel Roth and his wife Josephine.

#

"Look honey, our rivals!" chuckled Samuel.

#

Hugo was spooked his cousin surprised him by showing up at the soccer match on the other side. The entire plan would soon be ruined all because of Samuel's behavior.

#

Josephine's Concerns

#

Josephine could see that Hugo had a worried look on his face, even in his "Moshie" attire. The "Moshie" facade would soon unravel right in front of everyone.

#

"You're a fool for bringing us here" whispered Josephine.

#

"Where's your sense of exposure and adventure?" laughed Samuel, "It's not every now and then you get to surprise your main opponent at a sports event."

\#

"I don't care about that, I care about your scheme with using Hugo like this" said Josephine.

\#

Josephine had every right to feel worried for Hugo's own mental health, she could get a sense he was rather embarrassed in seeing Samuel. But Samuel wanted to keep on pressing the envelope even further with his cousin.

\#

"Let's just see where this goes, I feel like if I can embarrass a known Senator and his daughter I can win the election easily" continued Samuel.

\#

Josephine turned around, she couldn't believe her husband was so selfish in sacrificing his morals for an election.

\#

"I can't believe what sort of person you have become" sighed Josephine.

\#

Josephine didn't want to make too much of a big deal or it'd harm Hugo's own mental well being even further.

Chapter One

<u>Close Call</u>

\#

After the large television monitor showed Nia and "Moshie" on one end, and on the other Samuel and Josephine as the match soon ended Josephine slapped her husband.

\#

"You pulled a very risky move by showing up at the same event with Nia, how did you know she'd end up at this event?" asked Josephine.

\#

Josephine was getting curious to know how her husband had first-hand knowledge of the event. Samuel shrugged it off, giving the event being well-known as an alibi.

\#

"Hey, it's a well known event, I planned to show up for my campaign anyway" added Samuel.

\#

Josephine grumbled as she was heading towards the parking lot, she couldn't believe her husband was this callous towards Nia and Hugo. Josephine had a hunch her husband was doing something illegal but didn't know what it was. Samuel sighed with some relief, Benny along with the Jana brothers both text messaged him after seeing his image on the television monitor through social media.

\#

"What were you doing at that event, do you realize our operation could be compromised?" asked Dev.

\#

"I agree with my brother" said Ojas in a text message following Dev's, "you should have known better not to show up like that."

\#

"Hey, it builds character" said Samuel in a reply.

\#

Samuel had to keep his cool as he noticed Nia approaching him.

\#

Meeting Nia and "Moshie"

\#

Nia felt it was odd for her main opponent - Samuel Roth to show up at the same soccer event in the same stadium. It was more awkward for Hugo trying to pretend to be his persona "Moshie Scheinman".

\#

"So you must be Samuel Roth I have been hearing so much about" said Nia, "trying to take my father's position from me."

\#

"You know the people do not like it when legacy enters as an issue where family gets to receive the title of any given position" continued Samuel.

#

Samuel was firm with his beliefs on this, he hated seeing "legacy" political affiliations happening even in the Red, White and Secure.

#

"There's nothing illegal of what my campaign is doing" said Nia, "and I think you showed up at this event to try to upstage my new boyfriend."

#

Hugo waved at Samuel pretending as if he didn't know him.

#

"Uh, yea, very underhanded of you" added Hugo.

#

"Well Moshie" said Samuel with a wink to Hugo, "this event has been on my schedule list for sometime and since you two were going to show up, I just wanted to make an entrance to introduce myself to the both of you."

#

Samuel was purposely being sly around Nia and "Moshie", he was trying to make up for just surprising Hugo in that sense and fashion. However, Hugo could tell already Benny and the Jana brothers were not pleased with what transpired and even social media was on a blitz about the stunt.

\#

Samuel's Stunt

\#

Samuel Roth's stunt received social media attention, Benny who was in his hotel was taking notes over the matter. He sensed trouble with this "Moshie Scheinman" persona of Hugo Roth's. He was busy on a phone call with Zafar Mehmet who was in Las Vegas also observing everything.

\#

"This does not look good" said Zafar on the other line.

\#

"I do not disagree with you, Samuel did make too much of a bold move" continued Benny.

\#

Zafar still felt the scheme could be implemented in a way that Benny would get paid. The stunt already raised Samuel's popularity in the polls for the Georgian Senatorial race.

\#

"Well, the only good news is that Samuel's little stunt did raise his own popularity" continued Zafar, "but at his cousin's expense!"

#

"Just imagine if he's exposed as a fraud, Nia will go down with him" added Benny.

#

"That's true" continued Zafar, "the public hates dishonesty and liars."

#

Zafar sighed as he soon said goodbye to his friend Benny, Zafar sat back in his office chair in his mansion. He couldn't believe what was happening in the state of Georgia. He got a sense President Harold Truax might try to contact Benny soon after this, if he becomes a thorn in the Blue Eagle Collective's operations.

#

<u>Angry Josephine</u>

#

Back with the aftermath of the soccer event, Samuel soon headed towards his car where Josephine was sitting in the shotgun seat. She was rather unhappy with all of this.

#

"You shouldn't have shown yourself like that to the public" said Josephine as she began to nag.

#

Samuel was use to the nagging as he started the car and started to drive off.

#

"Well, I hate to say it, but you are going to be wrong" continued Samuel, "my popularity has gone up in the polls with that little stunt. I just need to figure out Nia's next moves."

#

"And how are you going to do that, are you a mind reader, do you read mines?" continued Josephine.

#

The nagging continued throughout the drive home, Samuel knew the Jana brothers were not happy with his surprise stunt. However, he took a glance over his cellphone and a few positive text messages came from them after the event was over.

#

"Poll numbers are showing you are gaining ground" said Dev in a text message.

#

"Rather surprising and very risky what you did" added Ojas in another text message.

#

The Jana brothers were perplexed by Samuel's unorthodox behavior, but perhaps the "Moshie Scheinman" persona did make up for all of that.

Chapter Two

Nia's Concert Suggestion

\#

Meanwhile back at Nia's apartment, Nia wanted to relax for a moment before she would think of something her new boyfriend would do. Hugo was rather nervous being in her apartment, even under his "Moshie" persona.

\#

"Moshie, how would you like to have a concert for my campaign?" asked Nia.

\#

Hugo paused for a moment.

\#

"Concert?" asked Hugo.

\#

"Yea, you told me on our date before we became official that you were into tours around the world" continued Nia.

\#

Hugo froze in terror, he had such stage fright. He couldn't believe Nia would suggest a statement like that. Surely he knew his cousin Samuel was listening in on all of this from the other end. So was Benny to a degree, Hugo swallowed as he turned towards Nia.

\#

"Sure, a concert for your campaign just give me the day and I will see what I can do" said Hugo.

\#

"Excellent, I will give my campaign manager the details along with my father I am sure they'd be thrilled" added Nia.

\#

Hugo soon swallowed again, he never organized a concert in all of his entire life.

\#

"Sure, I will try to see who I can get to help with my concert just state the time and place" continued Hugo.

\#

"Splendid, please make sure it's done by the end of the month" continued Nia.

\#

Nia gave Hugo a hug, Hugo couldn't help but to blush over this.

\#

<u>Getting Help from Benny</u>

#

Hugo soon promptly arrived back at his apartment, sweat ran down his forehead as he couldn't believe what sort of thing Nia suggested - a concert!

#

"I have to call Benny!" cried Hugo.

#

Hugo soon called up Benny Dubious, Benny wasn't pleased that Samuel nearly tried to ruin his own operation. A concert would be putting Hugo back in the limelight again in his "Moshie Scheinman" persona.

#

"She wants a what?!" cried Benny.

#

"A concert for her campaign" continued Hugo.

#

Benny grumbled, he knew Samuel already had the knowledge already on the sort of concert.

#

"Hang on for a moment, I might do some research on who are the known rabbis that could assist you" continued Benny.

#

Neither Samuel nor Hugo were religious Jews at all, but if word were to get out about Samuel's illegal activities with all of this it would also ruin Hugo's reputation as well. It would be bad either way if Hugo concerned his "Moshie" persona or if he didn't. Benny would have to figure out who among the rabbis would assist him in this endeavor, he would have to try his best knowing Hugo was on a schedule to get it done soon.

#

Benny Making a Few Calls

#

Although Hugo's "Moshie" persona was growing in popularity on social media, not that many rabbis have heard of the Jewish rapper known as "Moshie Scheinman", and not many of them were fond of social media.

#

"You are expecting me to waste time with a rapper who claims to be Jewish?" remarked one rabbi on the phone with Benny.

#

"But it's for Ms. Nia Carver's campaign" continued Benny.

#

"We are not interested" continued the rabbi.

#

It was mostly like that across Atlanta, Georgia, despite Hugo's persona being trendy on social media. Not that many among the religious clergy would assist Hugo on creating a concert for Nia. Until Benny came across two rabbis - Rabbi Isaac Green and Stephen Katz. They shared a synagogue together with the same congregation who were followers of Hugo's persona.

#

"Did you say you were affiliated with the Jewish rapper known as Moshie Scheinman?" asked Rabbi Isaac.

#

"Yep, uh, I know him through a friend" continued Benny.

#

"Both Stephen and I would love to assist you in helping you with a concert" continued Rabbi Isaac, "meet us at the deli in downtown Atlanta and we'll discuss our matters further with both of you."

#

Benny soon sent a text message to Hugo.

#

"I got the rabbis who would help us, but you owe me one" said Benny in the text message to Hugo.

#

Hugo sighed, he wondered if the rabbis would see right through him.

#

<u>The Deli Restaurant Meeting</u>

#

The two rabbis soon arranged the meeting between Benny and "Moshie", as they sat at the table waiting for the two to show up. They felt it was rather off of a Jewish rapper suddenly rising to fame.

#

"Doesn't it seem strange to you a Jewish rapper none of the other rabbis have ever heard regardless of their own Jewishness has ever heard of such a rapper?" asked Rabbi Stephen as he gazed at Rabbi Isaac.

#

"I know it sounds strange that this young man is rising on social media but let's just give him a chance" continued Rabbi Isaac.

#

Hugo arrived first before Benny in his "Moshie" attire persona. The two rabbis soon stood up and shook "Moshie's" hand, and gave him a hug.

#

"You must be that Jewish rapper who has been dating that Senatorial candidate" continued Rabbi Isaac.

#

"Uh, yes that's me" said Hugo.

\#

Soon Benny Dubious entered the deli, he gazed around the deli first and soon sat greeted the two rabbis.

\#

"And you must be Benny" said Rabbi Stephen as he firmly shook Benny's hand.

\#

"Now let's get down to business, the concert is said to take place here in downtown Atlanta, Georgia" continued Benny, "it's a way for Nia to boost her campaign."

\#

"Most of our congregation will be willing to vote for the Blue Eagle Collective" continued Rabbi Isaac, "we're just shocked to see a Jewish rapper already making headways."

\#

"So are your lyrics in English, Hebrew or Yiddish or a combination?" asked Rabbi Stephen.

\#

Hugo froze in fright, he hardly knew either of the two Jewish languages mentioned.

Chapter Three

<u>Fake It Til You Make It Again</u>

#

Hugo stood frozen solid as he sat down at the table with the two rabbis. He hardly knew either of the two Jewish languages - Hebrew and Yiddish.

#

"Our congregation speaks both of them fluently" continued Rabbi Isaac.

#

"What do we do, I don't speak those languages" whispered Hugo.

#

"Just remember fake it until you make it" whispered Benny.

#

Hugo soon changed his demeanor to feel more confident towards the two rabbis.

#

"Sure, uh, my lyrics are in all three languages" continued Hugo.

#

"That's terrific!" laughed Rabbi Isaac, "We could always use a rapper who is fluent in both Jewish languages on our synagogue."

#

Poor Hugo, he knew this was going to be one giant mess in the end for him and even for his cousin Samuel. Benny on the other hand had an ace up his sleeve to resolve this matter.

#

"We will organize the concert right here in downtown Atlanta, everyone will be welcome to it" added Benny.

#

"Good, just give us the time and day and we'll have our congregation members set everything up" added Rabbi Isaac.

#

The deal had been sealed between Benny and the two rabbis. Hugo knew he was going to be in big trouble if he didn't come up with any lyrics soon.

#

Hugo Panics

#

As the two rabbis left after they had their meals at the deli, Hugo was in panic mode with Benny.

#

"What do we do?!" cried Hugo, "I can't speak Yiddish or Hebrew and I'm hardly religious!"

\#

"Calm down, there is a way we can do this and get away with everything" continued Benny.

\#

Benny then thought of using AI, it was the only sort of tool left in the arsenal to save Hugo. This even with Benny's own run-in with an AI system that didn't seem to enjoy being abused with the Obeng family and their son Themba. Benny soon began to text message the Jana brothers on what to do.

\#

"Uh, I am going to need some help with helping Hugo and his little concert" continued Benny in a text message to both Dev and Ojas.

\#

"What can we do for you?" asked Dev.

\#

"I need an AI system that can create lyrics in English, Yiddish and Hebrew for Hugo" continued Benny in the text message.

\#

"That might sound hard for a task for even an AI system to do, but we'll figure it out" said Ojas.

#

The Jana brothers had the know-how to create their own AI system. The system itself would be ready before the concert.

#

<u>Happy Samuel</u>

#

Meanwhile for Samuel Roth, he was thrilled that Hugo continued to use his "Moshie" persona around Nia thinking that he was some kind of rapper. At the expense of his own personal mental health. Josephine didn't know how her husband knew everything in advance. Samuel had kept a few listening devices that Benny handed him in his den.

#

"How did you know about that soccer event that Nia and Hugo would be there?" asked Josephine.

#

"Hey, like I said before it's a widely known event" continued Samuel.

#

Samuel was thrilled that his stunt brought him up in the polls, he couldn't believe all of this was happening so fast. He received an message from President Harold Truax through an anonymous number congratulating him on his rise in popularity.

#

"I am very happy that you are doing so well" continued President Harold Truax in the text message.

#

The anonymous number was being used so that the former President couldn't be traced at all. Samuel no doubt was thrilled that he was going to beat Nia, all he would soon have to do is show up at her concert and watch her campaign collapse.

#

Upset Ashura

#

Not everyone was thrilled with the concert proposal by Nia Carver, her campaign manager in particular - Ashura Clark disagreed with the move. She was busy on the phone with Nia after she made the post on social media of a concert for her campaign involving "Moshie Scheinman".

#

"You are risking it by being out in the open like this" said Ashura, "this new boyfriend of yours is rather suspicious that he suddenly rises to fame like this."

#

"Listen, Ashura he's going to help me catch up to Samuel" continued Nia.

#

"Well, it better not backfire on you" continued Ashura, "events like the elementary school and even that soccer match were better than this."

\#

Ashura also was surprised to see Samuel at the event with his wife.

\#

"I am just worried that Samuel is spying on you in some manner" continued Ashura.

\#

Nia laughed it off, she couldn't believe someone as incompetent like Samuel Roth could do such an illegal activity.

\#

"Please, my opponent wouldn't be able to do that" said Nia.

\#

Ashura knew otherwise, she got the feeling Nia's father - Senator Amos Carver III also felt something was off with "Moshie".

Part Two

Chapter Four

<u>The Senator's Concerns</u>

\#

Ashura decided to call Senator Amos Carver III, she was determine that she got the feeling that he agreed with her on the matter of both "Moshie" and the concert.

\#

"This is Senator Amos Carver speaking" said Senator Amos.

\#

Senator Amos was in his office in downtown Atlanta when he answered the call. He could tell it was urgent since it was from Nia's campaign manager.

\#

"Sir, I don't agree with this concert that your daughter is planning with her new boyfriend" continued Ashura.

\#

"I do not disagree with your sentiment" continued Senator Amos, "I can't say that much but I have someone working on the case of who Moshie's true identity could be."

\#

The Senator was right to keep everything hush, hush for the time being. He received a text message from Agent GA over the license plate of "Moshie's" car.

\#

"Our researchers did the analysis of the license plate and who the owner of the car is" said Agent GA.

\#

"So who could it be?" asked Senator Amos as he sent a text message back.

\#

"Hugo Roth" continued Agent GA.

\#

"Wait, the Hugo Roth, the cousin of the notorious Samuel Roth my daughter's opponent?!" said Senator Amos in a text message reply.

\#

The Senator was quite perplexed to how Hugo Roth managed to make up a name in thin air at the event at the elementary school.

\#

<u>**Sounding the Alarm to Ashura**</u>

\#

The Senator called Ashura again, this time she knew it was urgent.

\#

"Yes Senator?" asked Ashura.

\#

"Moshie Scheinman is really Hugo Roth in disguise" continued Senator Amos, "I don't want to reveal the source who told me, but the license plate matches Hugo Roth's car!"

\#

Ashura froze, she couldn't believe how compromised Nia's campaign had become!

\#

"I will try to break it to Nia" continued Ashura.

\#

The Senator thought about his daughter's feelings for "Moshie" and paused for a moment.

\#

"Don't, she needs to learn this lesson on her own" continued Senator Amos.

\#

"But she could lose to someone like Samuel Roth!" cried Ashura.

\#

The Senator sighed.

#

"I know it sounds hard, but believe me, everything will make sense in the end even if she does somehow make it" added Senator Amos.

#

The Senator soon ends the call, Ashura was in shock that someone like Hugo Roth to pull it all off. The only one who was clueless on the matter was Nia, she was still busy trying to text message "Moshie" back and forth through a profile that Hugo had created on social media.

#

Keeping the "Moshie" Persona Going

#

In the meantime, while Hugo waited for the rabbis to get their congregation to organize the concert and the Jana brothers to get the AI program for him to use to make up the lyrics with. He was busy text messaging Nia back and forth.

#

"Moshie, you are so wonderful!" said Nia in one text message.

#

"Yea, I am glad you like me" added Hugo in a reply.

#

Hugo had no choice but to lead Nia on with this persona, it was his only choice left. He just couldn't reveal the real him.

#

"I am so happy that you are going to have a concert for my campaign" said Nia in another text message.

#

"Yes, very excited" added Hugo.

#

Sweat ran down Hugo's forehead as he continued to send text messages to Nia throughout the evening. He soon had to rest, but as Hugo soon headed to bed, he soon found himself in a large stage. There were so many people there that there were too many heads to count. He was already in his "Moshie Scheinman" persona, ready for the concert to move forward.

#

The Dream Concert Nightmare

#

Hugo always hated being around large number of crowds, especially if he was going to be the center of attention.

#

"MOSHIE, MOSHIE, MOSHIE!" roared the dream crowd of people before him.

#

Everything was so loud and wild before him, it was pandemonium! Banners of Nia Hope Carver were in droves in the sea of dream people before him. On the stage was Benny Dubious wheeling out some sort of strange computer system.

#

"This is the computer system for your lyrics" whispered Benny.

#

The dream Benny soon handed over Hugo a microphone, all Hugo had to do was just say a few words but instead of those words, the AI computer system would produce a song in either English, Yiddish or Hebrew. The dream version of Benny Dubious chuckled, he laughed at poor Hugo being so nervous. Then the crowd in the dream soon turned against Hugo.

#

"FRAUD, FRAUD, FRAUD!" bellowed the dream crowd.

#

Objects were thrown at poor Hugo, he had to hid behind the computer console that the dream Benny had rolled out. No one was coming to help Hugo in the dream, everyone knew he was going to become a laughing stalk!

#

<u>Frighten Hugo</u>

#

Hugo woke up from his nightmare sweating all over his body. He couldn't believe the sort of nightmare he had just experienced. He HATED large crowds if he had to be the one to give a speech or worse write a song.

#

"Why did I make up that name!" cried Hugo.

#

Hugo grumbled in bed as he began to struggle the moral grasp of the situation. He couldn't believe he was fooling everyone on social media with his "Moshie Scheinman" persona. Then he gazed at his cellphone and noticed a text message was sent by Samuel.

#

"So happy for your little concert, I can't wait to be part of the crowd" said Samuel in the text message.

#

Roth suddenly realized this is what his cousin Samuel wanted! His cousin wanted to ruin Nia's campaign with a fake boyfriend! At first, Samuel just wanted to see if Nia had any scandals, then Hugo had to open his mouth and make up a name. Hugo rolled back in bed, he wasn't going to get out at all.

#

"She's going to hate me, everyone's going to hate me!" cried Hugo.

#

Hugo was clearly in agony over this, but suddenly a strange envelope slipped right through his mail slot. As Hugo gazed upon it, he noticed it was some sort of strange letter from a certain "Agent GA".

Chapter Five

Agent GA's Letter

\#

Hugo froze at the letter, he couldn't believe the Blue Eagle Collective were watching him the entire time. He slowly began to open the letter and soon read the message.

\#

"Dear Hugo Roth, I know why you are trying to pretend to be Moshie Scheinman. Not out to help your cousin Samuel Roth and his election campaign. If you have any moral issues about it, you can always discuss these matters with me. Please meet me at the coffee shop. Sincerely Agent GA."

\#

Hugo knew he had to be brave, he soon decided he was going to go out as "Moshie Scheinman" to meet this Agent GA. As he put on his clothes and headed off towards the coffee shop, it took him just a few minutes to get there. When he arrived, there was Agent GA sitting at a table with another chair waiting.

\#

"Please have a seat" said Agent GA.

\#

Hugo knew he was in big trouble with the Blue Eagle Collective, they had spies all over the country and it was a bigger group than the CIA and the FBI put together.

#

"So you figured out who I am?" asked Hugo as he sat down.

#

"Yes" said Agent GA, "I have, but I will not say that much to ruin your reputation. I'm a professional after all."

#

Hugo knew he needed help to get out of this mess.

#

Agent GA's Suggestions

#

Agent GA sighed as he gazed at Hugo, he was keeping his own identity a secret from him.

#

"I have a few suggestions to make" said Agent GA, "seeing how you didn't have any ill-intention for Ms. Nia and you really like her, I would try to admit it prior to the concert."

#

"But what if she feels devastated?" asked Hugo.

\#

"If she feels devastated, angry, mad, whatever that's on her end" continued Agent GA, "you can try to use the concert to embarrass your own cousin Samuel."

\#

Hugo thought of outing Samuel as a way to ruin his own operation against Nia.

\#

"I know this seems all too much to intake" continued Agent GA, "but it'd make sense once the time has come."

\#

Hugo thought about all of the illegal activities his cousin Samuel was getting away. Wiretapping his opponent's apartment was one of those illegal activities, and even the concert itself was fraud on his end.

\#

"I will think about it" said Hugo.

\#

"Yes, please do" said Agent GA.

\#

The Blue Eagle spy sat back at continued to sip his coffee as Hugo soon got up and left.

\#

Hugo's Moral Struggle

\#

Hugo soon headed towards his car and drove off, he couldn't shake the feeling on what Agent GA told him.

\#

"Samuel is going way too far with all of this" thought Hugo in his own head.

\#

Suddenly as Hugo continued to drive, a ghost of "Moshie Scheinman" appeared. However this "ghost" was really Hugo's own "Moshie" persona speaking to him.

\#

"Everyone is going to think you're a fraud if you reveal the truth about me" said Moshie.

\#

Hugo glanced at the Moshie persona of himself, he ignored it as he continued onward back to his apartment. The "ghost" of his persona was trying to egg Hugo to continue the persona for Samuel.

\#

"Do it for your cousin, you promised him after all" said Moshie as he was right behind Hugo.

\#

"You're not real!" bellowed Hugo.

\#

"But I am real, everyone thinks I am real" said Moshie.

\#

Hugo waved his hands in front of him and the ghost of his persona vanished before him. There was quite much fear in Hugo, he couldn't believe his "Moshie" persona was getting out of hand. He had to end it at the concert.

\#

AI System Ready

\#

As Hugo attempted to rest after that strange meeting with Agent GA, his cellphone soon buzzed and it was Benny Dubious on the other end.

\#

"The Jana brothers are finished with the AI system, they just want to test it out" said Benny.

\#

Hugo was surprised at how fast the Jana brothers - Dev and Ojas worked on the AI system. Benny soon sent a text message to the Jana brothers' residence and soon Hugo was once again on the road. Hugo did his best trying to maintain control, he got a sense his "Moshie" ghost persona was in the back seat of his car.

\#

"Remember, I am always watching" laughed Moshie.

\#

"You're not real, get out of my head!" cried Hugo.

\#

Hugo did his best trying to ignore the ghostly persona, it only vanished as Hugo arrived at the Jana brother's residence which was just a single story house. Benny was already waiting for him.

\#

"I can't believe those Jana brothers are fast" said Benny.

\#

Benny soon showed Hugo inside, he could tell Hugo was having moral issues over the complexity of his "Moshie" persona.

\#

"Still feeling all that sort of trouble?" asked Benny.

\#

Hugo nodded.

\#

"Well if you just want to get through with it remember fake it until you make it" continued Benny.

#

Benny then showed Hugo towards where the Jana brothers were waiting.

#

The Song Writing Computer

#

Hugo froze as he entered one of the rooms where the computer console was ready. It looked exactly like the dream version of it!

#

"Amazing isn't it?" asked Dev.

#

"All you have to do is just say whatever words in the microphone and the AI system will randomly select either English, Yiddish or Hebrew and speak it" said Ojas.

#

"Go ahead, try it" said Dev.

#

Hugo walked up towards the microphone he gazed at what it would be his audience. Suddenly the stage fright kicked in, sure there was no body there, but Hugo was still frighten nonetheless.

#

"I, I can't do it" said Hugo, "I have too much stage fright!"

#

Benny soon planted his palm on his face, he knew Hugo had to get over his stage fright.

#

"Looks like you have more problems than just speaking to women" added Benny.

#

Benny decided to test out the microphone, immediately as Benny spoke the computer AI system wrote a song in Yiddish. No one in the room could understand the song.

#

"Hmm, maybe we should download a few of the songs and post them on social media, leave that to me" said Benny.

#

Hugo knew this would just bring further trouble for him.

Chapter Six

<u>Uploading the Songs</u>

#

Now the AI computer didn't seem to care whose voice it was that said the words. It would just simply create a random song from any of the three languages. Yiddish was the first language selected. Benny laughed as he heard his own voice in that language.

#

"Let's see if social media would like this" laughed Benny.

#

Benny uploaded the song file to Hugo's "Moshie" social media account.

#

"A preview of what's to come" said the post.

#

Benny soon posts it on a laptop that the Jana brothers had laid out. Already people were buying into the music. And again the "Moshie Scheinman" persona soon began to grow in popularity. Hugo nearly freaked out over this matter, he knew it was going too far with this.

#

"Wow, a preview for the upcoming concert next week!" said a male user.

#

"I can't wait!" added a female user.

#

Those on social media went a blaze with the "Moshie" persona despite it being Benny's voice stating the lyrics through the AI system in Yiddish. But no one could really tell if it was Benny's or Hugo's since it was generated by an AI system.

#

Confident Benny

#

Benny glared at Hugo, he could still get the feeling that Hugo lacked confidence in the "Moshie" persona.

#

"I see you still lack confidence" said Benny as he got up.

#

The Jana brothers could see it as well, they wondered if all of this could backfire and make matters worse for Samuel.

#

"Either this could help or hurt Samuel, I can't tell at this moment" said Dev.

#

"Me neither, but so long as Hugo isn't confident there is no way this would work" added Ojas.

\#

"Well it has to work, and I will have to be the one to build that confidence again" said Benny.

\#

Benny wanted to head to Hugo's apartment to have Hugo dawn the "Moshie" persona attire again. Hugo couldn't believe all of this was happening.

\#

"Uh, I guess we'd have to just get this over with" sighed Hugo.

\#

"That's the spirit" said Benny.

\#

Benny followed Hugo to his car and soon got into the back seat. Hugo drove off, he was quite nervous. The "Moshie" persona was haunting him as a "ghost", invisible to Benny as the persona sat next to him.

\#

"Ha, you're nervous" laughed Moshie.

\#

Hugo continued to concentrate on driving back to his apartment.

\#

<u>Practicing with "Moshie"</u>

\#

It took Hugo about a few minutes to get back to his apartment, there Benny got out and followed Hugo up towards his apartment. As they arrived, Hugo soon began to get dressed in his "Moshie Scheinman" attire.

\#

"You need to practice on pretending you are reading those lyrics" said Benny, "what's the definition I am looking for, oh yea lip singing. You need to practice to lip sing!"

\#

"But I don't have a microphone with me" said Hugo.

\#

"Use your cellphone" continued Benny.

\#

Hugo sighed, his cellphone was the next best thing to a microphone. Hugo continued to practice with Benny on his lip singing routine. It seemed like hours had passed, but it only had been a few minutes. Benny clearly could get the feeling Hugo was struggling still with all of this.

\#

"You really do not enjoy this for your cousin?" asked Benny.

#

Hugo sighed, he knew Benny wouldn't like his answer.

#

"How would you feel if you were forced to do something immoral that you couldn't live with yourself?" asked Hugo.

#

Benny never thought of anything like that, he was only after the money from the Red, White and Secure.

#

Caring About Money Over Morals

#

Benny Dubious was clearly motivated over money to get this job done rather than morals.

#

"I would counter your claim with fake it until you make it" continued Benny.

#

Benny was very firm in this belief, it got him so far ahead that he was now running his own casino in Las Vegas. He wasn't about to give it up, or let someone who cared too much about morality get in his path.

#

"But everyone will hate you for it" said Hugo.

#

"That's the price it comes" continued Benny, "this Moshie Scheinman sounds exactly like me on so many levels, and he has so much potential. Which is why social media is going crazy for him!"

#

"But they all believing in lies" continued Hugo.

#

Benny laughed it all off.

#

"That's just the way life is" continued Benny, "sometimes life isn't fair, and those who know how to work around the unfairness have to be unfair themselves!"

#

Hugo just knew he had to stop this at the concert, Benny along with his cousin were going too far in their quest for money and power. But Hugo would sadly have to play along with them.

Chapter Seven

After Practice with Benny

#

Benny soon left Hugo's apartment, Hugo slumped down in a chair wondering what to do next. He then glanced over and noticed "Moshie Scheinman" or at least the ghost of the persona glancing back at him.

#

"Hey, I am exactly like Benny, your friend is right about me" said Moshie.

#

Hugo refused to respond to the persona.

#

"So you are giving me the silent treatment instead of accepting me as part of you" continued Moshie, "you know you are just as guilty as Benny and Samuel in this scheme of a mess."

#

Moshie or at least the ghost of the persona was right on cue to Hugo's own moral struggle.

#

"You're right, I am part of this mess, but I can fix this mess" added Hugo, "by telling the truth."

\#

Moshie laughed at his original counterpart self.

\#

"You think even by telling the truth I will just disappear, vanish, go away just like that?" asked Moshie.

\#

"It's worth a try" continued Hugo, "I am not a liar."

\#

"But you did lie to a Senator and to his daughter, and you're dating her!" laughed Moshie.

\#

Hugo grumbled and then took off his hoodie and threw it at the ghost who then vanished. He knew he had to get out of this very soon or things will escalate quickly in all the wrong ways.

\#

<u>Setting Up the Concert</u>

\#

The days went by, and Hugo continued to practice lip singing with Benny Dubious. The concert's day was soon arriving. A few days prior to the concert, Rabbis Isaac Green and Stephen Katz and their congregation were constructing the stage that "Moshie Scheinman" would be on display. There was much excitement going around the city, and even on social media.

#

"I can't wait until this concert is over" said Rabbi Stephen.

#

"Why, you're not the one who is going on stage, you don't have stage fright" laughed Rabbi Isaac.

#

"I know, but the costs of making sure the concert goes off without a hitch is pretty expensive" added Rabbi Stephen.

#

The members of the congregation were part of the construction crew, moving and building the parts of the concert together. There were members of the Blue Eagle Collective spies as security for the concert so that nothing else were to go wrong. Ms. Ashura Clark, Nia's campaign manager had her doubts about the concert. She was busy meeting up with the two rabbis responsible for it.

#

"It's so nice to meet you" said Rabbi Isaac as he gave her a hug.

#

"Yes it is, any friend of the host is a friend of ours" added Rabbi Stephen.

\#

"You both know I do not approve of the concert, despite it being approved by Nia" said Ashura.

\#

"What's there not to go wrong with?" asked Rabbi Isaac.

\#

Ashura knew the rabbis wouldn't like what she had to say on "Moshie".

\#

Ashura's Concerns on "Moshie" and the Concert

\#

Ashura took note on how expensive the concert was getting, even if the rabbis and their congregation were the ones building everything. She got some sense that this "Moshie" was a fraud and something bad was going to happen at the concert.

\#

"I am just doing my duty as campaign manager to make sure this concert is safe for the candidate" continued Ashura.

\#

"With all due respect, we respect everyone in the city" continued Rabbi Isaac.

\#

"And I also think this so-called Jewish rapper is a fake" continued Ashura.

#

The two rabbis laughed at this.

#

"Are you certain, a song came out in Yiddish on social media" added Rabbi Stephen.

#

The rabbis pulled up the post that Benny had posted earlier on social media. There was a song in Yiddish alright, but no one could figure out it was done by an AI computer system.

#

"Hmm, that does seem legit" said Ashura as she took a glance at the song file.

#

"You worry too much" said Rabbi Isaac, "let us handle everything for the concert. You just have to show up with Nia, her boyfriend being on stage and her father."

#

The rabbis were no doubt thrilled that the day of the concert was approaching.

#

<u>A Word with Nia</u>

\#

"Moshie Scheinman" strangely didn't want to look at the concert as it was being built. Hugo obviously was paranoid it would look too similar like the concert in his dream. But Nia didn't know that as she was taking a glance of all of the construction.

\#

"Ms. Carver, a word?" asked Ashura as she approached Nia.

\#

"Yes, what's your concerns?" asked Nia.

\#

"What if this Moshie Scheinman isn't who he say she is and is just a fraud?" asked Ashura.

\#

"Don't be silly, no one would just make up a name and try to impress me" laughed Nia.

\#

But Nia was dead wrong on all of this, she didn't realize how much of a compromised campaign she was running. The entire stunt with the concert could really break her campaign altogether. Ashura knew this, and she also felt Nia's father - Senator Amos knew this as well.

\#

"I am just saying everything and anything can go wrong" said Ashura, "I am just trying to look out for you."

#

Nia took note on Ashura's word, but felt nothing bad would happen. She then received a text message from "Moshie".

#

"I will be looking at the concert hall tomorrow when it's finished" said Hugo in the text message using Moshie's image on social media.

Part Three

75

Chapter Eight

"Moshie" Inspects the Concert

\#

The following day, the concert for "Moshie" was finished. Hugo soon arrived in his car in his "Moshie Scheinman" attire and parked on the street. He then got out and noticed the concert. To Hugo's horror, it looked exactly like the concert in his dream!

\#

"What the—?!" cried Hugo.

\#

Before Hugo could use a swear word, Rabbi Isaac soon emerged with Rabbi Stephen, and a few construction workers.

\#

"Do you like our concert that we built for you?" asked Rabbi Stephen.

\#

Hugo didn't want to say anything back to the two rabbis, he could tell they and their congregation had worked very hard.

\#

"We built this with our own sweat and blood" said a male congregation member.

\#

"Yep, and we're willing to root for Ms. Nia Carver at the concert" added a female congregation member.

\#

Hugo froze in terror, there was no way of turning back from all of this. It was going to happen in just a few days.

\#

"Uh, I just wanted to say you all did a bang up job" said Hugo.

\#

Hugo tried to have a smile on his face, he could tell the persona ghost of "Moshie" was right behind him.

\#

The "Moshie Ghost" Encourages Hugo

\#

Moshie Scheinman or at least the ghost of the persona was right behind Hugo preventing him to flee.

\#

"You have to do this, you got yourself in this mess" whispered Moshie.

\#

"I just wanted to say you all did such a wonderful, wonderful, wonderful job" said Hugo.

\#

Everyone cheered with excitement.

#

"We're very happy with how you feel" said Rabbi Isaac, "we look forward to the concert day where everything will go off without a hitch."

#

"Uh, yes, sure, without a hitch" added Hugo.

#

The rabbis could detect some nervousness on part of "Moshie", but then shrugged it off thinking it was just a natural reaction.

#

"Anyway, see you at the concert on Saturday" added Rabbi Stephen.

#

Hugo swallowed, the Moshie ghost persona soon vanished allowing him to leave the venue. As he headed towards his car, he soon received an anonymous text message from Agent GA.

#

"My boys and girls saw you at the concert area" said Agent GA in the text message, "meet me at the coffee shop and we can discuss these matters if you'd like."

#

Hugo sighed as he got into his car and drove off.

#

<u>Second Meeting with Agent GA</u>

#

Hugo soon arrived at the coffee shop, he still had his "Moshie Schein-man" attire on when he got out of the car. As he headed over to the coffee shop, he soon sat down in the same seat that was pulled up to him by Agent GA.

#

"Nice to see you again" said Agent GA.

#

"If you know my real identity why don't you just reveal it to the public?" asked Hugo.

#

"And ruin all of the fun against your cousin, ha" laughed Agent GA.

#

Agent GA knew that it was going to be Hugo and only Hugo to tell the truth to the crowds of people who were getting ready to go to the concert. The truth would always set them free, even if they'd certainly expose "Moshie Scheinman" as a fraud.

#

"Your cousin must have also planted listening devices in Nia's apartment complex" added Agent GA, "I already know this because there is going to be a search warrant to be issued against him. I know I am not supposed to tell, but I am only telling you because I think you are honest."

#

"Would anything happen to Benny or the others involved?" asked Hugo.

#

"Your cousin is all we want" said Agent GA, "we have other ways of handling Benny."

#

"What do you mean by other ways?" asked Hugo.

#

"That's only for Benny to find out" laughed Agent GA.

#

<u>Concerns for Benny and the Others</u>

#

Even though Benny Dubious tried to teach Hugo to become as dishonest as him, Hugo still couldn't shake the feeling on what the Blue Eagle Collective would do to Benny.

#

"I still want to know what you mean by that statement on Benny" added Hugo.

#

The agent glanced at Hugo and didn't say a word at first.

#

"You really do not want to know" continued Agent GA, "Benny Dubious has been a thorn in our operations since trying to help Mayor Bertha Sole back when he was the right-hand man of Khalid Jared Muhammad. He also meddled into the affairs of Mayor Ted Otenio, the current Mayor of Los Angeles."

#

Hugo paused for a moment.

#

"But that still doesn't mean you'd just go after him" added Hugo.

#

"Ted was brought into this country with one of our spies through Fritz Hans, Ted's uncle" continued Agent GA, "my counterparts Agent CA and NV have been discussing matters on what to do about Benny."

#

"I understand Benny is a disrupter" added Hugo, "but you still shouldn't take things to extreme."

#

"That all depends on what you'd do on the matter of the concert" continued Agent GA, "help Samuel and Benny will be a definite target in the near future."

#

Hugo knew Agent GA wasn't the man he was telling him, and soon had to leave.

Chapter Nine

<u>Morally Corrupt Society</u>

#

Hugo left the coffee shop and soon began to drive back to his apartment. The "Moshie" persona ghost soon appeared in the shotgun seat.

#

"Even the Blue Eagle Collective are highly as dishonest as those in the Red, White and Secure" continued Moshie, "if you go as me and continue my persona, I will be around you forever."

#

"Forever sounds like a long time" said Hugo.

#

"It is, and it's thanks to our morally corrupt society" said Moshie.

#

"Moshie" was no doubt being the Devil towards Hugo in trying to encourage the persona to continue.

#

"You know all things come to an end, even to a persona like yourself?" asked Hugo.

#

"Yes, I suppose, but only by your own choice" continued Moshie.

\#

The "Moshie" ghost soon vanishes as Hugo arrives back home. Hugo soon receives a text message from Nia through a social media account.

\#

"I am so happy that we're together, I hope to see you as a front row seat of the concert" said Nia.

\#

"Yes, me too" added Hugo as he sent a text message back.

\#

Hugo sighed, as he soon headed inside his apartment. He then fell face first onto the sofa.

\#

<u>Getting Ready for the Concert</u>

\#

While Hugo was resting for the rest of the day before the concert, the Jana brothers arrived with Benny on the stage of the concert. The Jana brothers had their computer console with them.

\#

"We're going to use this to make sure Hugo will say and do everything necessary to get through this" added Benny.

#

Dev found a plug to power the computer, and soon the computer itself was activated.

#

"Hey, just what is that on stage?" asked a male Blue Eagle spy.

#

"Uh, it's to help Moshie Scheinman it's an instrument he needs on the stage" said Benny.

#

"Well that works for me, best wishing him luck when he arrives tomorrow" said the male Blue Eagle spy.

#

The Blue Eagle spies would watch over the computer console to make sure no one would try to steal it. Benny could see the computer turn on like a charm.

#

"I must say, you guys did a great job in making sure this works out" said Benny.

#

"Yes, all in a days work" added Dev.

#

"I just hope our boss will be in the audience to witness everything" added Ojas.

\#

"I am sure he will" added Benny.

\#

Benny wanted to inform Samuel on the operation.

\#

Informing Samuel

\#

Benny took some photos of the computer console with his cellphone and then showed it to Samuel.

\#

"Everything is ready to go boss" said Benny.

\#

Samuel glanced at the photos on his cellphone.

\#

"Ha, President Harold Truax would be very pleased once the concert is messed up" laughed Samuel.

\#

Samuel did his best trying to keep quiet about the concert, his wife Josephine was already onto him.

#

"What was that dear about the upcoming concert in downtown?" asked Josephine, "You better not be dragging me there to just embarrass your opposition."

#

"But we're going to have a fun, fun time there dear" said Samuel.

#

Josephine sighed, she knew her husband was up to something suspicious but couldn't figure out what it was. Samuel then went back to looking at the photos and making comments on them to Benny.

#

"Well the boss approves of all of this" said Benny to Dev and Ojas.

#

"Yes, that's very good" said Ojas, "I sure hope he will watch everything unfold."

#

The Jana brothers already could get the feeling that the "Moshie Scheinman" persona would be exposed. But they didn't realize that Hugo himself was already planning to do the exposure.

#

<u>**Morning of the Concert**</u>

\#

The morning of the concert had already arrived and Hugo Roth soon got out of bed. He soon began to put on his "Moshie Scheinman" attire. The ghost of "Moshie" himself gave the thumbs up.

\#

"Like a mirror image" laughed Moshie.

\#

The ghost of Moshie began to follow Hugo throughout his apartment as he was trying to have breakfast. Though this wasn't a paranormal ghost at all, Moshie was still floating about and making degrading comments.

\#

"She is definitely going to hate you after today is done" laughed Moshie, "you can tell that women do not like to be led like this."

\#

"No, no they do not" sighed Hugo.

\#

"I also understand you have met this Agent GA, he won't do a single thing to help you either" added Moshie.

\#

Hugo ignored the Moshie ghost, until he left the apartment where the ghost of the persona soon vanished. Hugo then got into his car and soon headed off to first meet with Nia at her apartment. He could get the feeling this was going to be a very, very long day. At Nia's apartment, Nia was excited that she was going to be picked up by her boyfriend to go to the concert.

Chapter Ten

<u>Exciting Time</u>

#

Nia got dressed, in her concert attire. She then had her breakfast. She received a text message from Ashura, her campaign manager trying to urge her one more time to cancel the concert.

#

"You still have time to say no to the concert" continued Ashura in the text message, "I do not like this idea of so many people. It's not like a campaign rally which is more controlled."

#

"Please, lighten up, Moshie is going to be the main star of attraction" added Nia as she sent the text message back.

#

Soon Nia got the message from "Moshie" on his social media account.

#

"Here to pick you up" said Hugo in the text message.

#

"I will come out after I am finished breakfast" added Nia.

#

After Nia finished breakfast, and brushed her teeth she soon emerged from her apartment. She then headed towards Hugo's car and the two drove off together. Nia was so happy she was with the love of her life.

\#

"I am so excited that I'm going to get front row seat of your concert!" laughed Nia.

\#

Nia was filled with joy, she didn't think at all this was a compromising situation to be in.

\#

<u>Driving to the Concert</u>

\#

Traffic was already building up as Hugo made his way to downtown, Atlanta. He could see so many people all over the state were eager to see this Jewish rapper - "Moshie Scheinman". They didn't realize he was stuck in the middle of traffic with them.

\#

"Wow, so many people!" laughed Nia.

\#

"Yea, I am surprised they're all here for the concert" added Hugo.

\#

"They're all here for you, and will help me get past Samuel Roth" added Nia.

#

Hugo did his best trying not to be too nervous, as the traffic moved forward, the couple arrived a little ahead of schedule. Hugo found a parking spot, and paid for the parking service. He and Nia soon got out of the car and headed over towards the concert. Rows of Blue Eagle spies were around as security aside from the regular police.

#

"Right this way Mr. Moshie" said a female Blue Eagle spy.

#

The Blue Eagle spies escorted "Moshie" and Nia into the concert hall where they met Rabbis Isaac and Stephen.

#

"Moshie, Nia, you both made it" said Rabbi Isaac as he gave them both hugs and kisses.

#

"We both wish you the best of luck with this concert" said Rabbi Stephen.

#

Hugo soon headed towards the main area of the concert just to get a glimpse of it.

#

<u>Just Like the Nightmare!</u>

#

Hugo gazed at the concert and noticed the seats were slowly being filled in by those in the public. It was turning out just to be like his nightmare!

#

"I can't do this" thought Hugo in his own head.

#

"Sure you can" whispered Moshie.

#

Moshie, in his ghostly persona soon appeared right behind him. Yes, the very persona that was egging Hugo on.

#

"But so many people will think I am a fraud" added Hugo.

#

"Which is all the more reason why you should continue" whispered Moshie.

#

In the back stage area of the concert, Nia was confused on who Hugo was speaking to. No one was really there.

\#

"You should come in" said Nia.

\#

Nia could tell that "Moshie" had some stage fright.

\#

"Feeling nervous?" asked Nia.

\#

"Uh, a little" said Hugo.

\#

Hugo was about to rest from that dreadful experience when Senator Amos Carver III arrived with Ms. Ashura Clark. Much to Ashura's disapproval, she decided to show support for Nia.

\#

"I am doing this for Nia, not for the silly concert" added Ashura to Hugo and the two rabbis.

\#

"Just wish you the best of luck" said Senator Amos to Hugo.

\#

The Senator could tell this "Moshie" was way off, not who he seemed. Agent GA was onto the case but wanted it to come from the horse's mouth.

#

<u>Nearing Airtime</u>

#

Time was ticking away for Hugo to think of something. Either get on stage and perform or expose his cousin Samuel for the fraud that he really is. Either option sounded like a terrible idea!

#

"On the one hand, I would be ostracized by family" said Hugo to himself in his head, "on the other hand I would be ostracized by the love of my life!"

#

Hugo was clearly torn between his love for Ms. Nia Carver and the aspirations of his cousin - Samuel Roth. He could see Samuel in the distance in the audience. Samuel and his wife Josephine were attending the concert way in the back. Benny Dubious was also in the back end with Samuel along with the Jana brothers.

#

"Dear, who are these three men with you?" asked Josephine.

#

Josephine was getting suspicious on who Benny Dubious was, but wondered what were the Jana brothers doing at the concert.

#

"They're, uh business friends" continued Samuel, "I invited them to come to the concert with us."

#

Josephine sighed with a humpf as she turned against the trio.

#

"Pleasure to meet you Ms. Josephine Roth" said Benny as he was trying to be polite.

#

"Likewise" added Dev.

#

"As am I" added Ojas.

Epilogue

<u>Stage Fright Again!</u>

\#

Clearly there was still some stage fright in Hugo as he gazed out at the crowd before him. He could see so many unrecognizable faces in the crowd. It reminded him too much like the dream he had or should we say nightmare.

\#

"Do this" whispered Moshie.

\#

The ghost of the persona was whispering in Hugo's ears to go forward with this. Agent GA who had arrived in the back area of the concert could see how Hugo was struggling to move forward.

\#

"Come on kid, reveal the truth about your cousin" added Agent GA.

\#

It was so much of a mental trauma going inside of Hugo, Hugo needed more time on his hand to prepare for all of this.

\#

"Excuse me for one moment" said Hugo as he soon headed off stage.

\#

Hugo could see Agent GA was there in the back stage waiting for him.

\#

"Listen, you have to go forward with this, there is no escaping this" added Agent GA.

\#

"I know there isn't but so many people will be disappointed" added Hugo.

\#

"They will, but it'd soon make sense to all of them, anger will only be short lived" added Agent GA.

\#

The agent was trying to comfort Hugo before going on stage. Hugo was going to make the big introduction.

\#

"Moshie's" Entrance

\#

Hugo slowly emerged on stage again, the crowd could see this "Moshie" wasn't who he seemed to be.

\#

"Hey, I came to hear songs in the promised languages!" cried one man in the crowd.

\#

"Sorry, sorry for keeping you all waiting like that and wondering off" said Hugo as he took the microphone.

\#

The audience cheered "Moshie's" name.

\#

"MOSHIE, MOSHIE, MOSHIE!" bellowed the crowd.

\#

Even Samuel who was in the back row of the concert couldn't believe he could pull it off. It could go both ways - either he could be exposed on stage or Nia could be ruined!

\#

"Dear, is there something you are not telling me, why does that figure look so much like—" said Josephine as she gasped "—HUGO!"

\#

Josephine angrily turned towards her husband, she then turned towards his business friends Benny and the Jana brothers.

\#

"You did this to him?" asked Josephine.

\#

"Hey, he made up his name all on his own" continued Samuel, "that's all on him and not me."

#

"That portion of it is true" added Benny.

#

"Well I want one of you to retrieve him or I will ruin your Senate campaign myself" added Josephine.

#

Josephine was serious about trying to pull Hugo from the venue, and Benny sighed that he would have to be the one to do it.

#

<u>Rescue Attempt?</u>

#

Benny sighed, he knew it was going to be his job to retrieve poor Hugo Roth from having the embarrassment of going forward with the concert.

#

"Okay, I guess I will be the one to do this since I did teach him to lip sing after all" added Benny.

#

"Yea, Benny will do it" laughed Samuel.

#

"He better" said Josephine.

#

Josephine didn't want Hugo to go through anymore trauma than he already had. Benny did his best trying to make his way through the crowd, but rows of people were blocking his path.

#

"Well, the first song for today is going to be in" said Hugo as he began to say words in the microphone.

#

Hugo turned on the computer and soon Hebrew popped up as the first language.

#

"Hebrew" said Hugo.

#

The song had a strange buzz to it as poor Benny was doing his best trying to make his way through the crowd of people. Would Benny Dubious be successful in rescuing Hugo? Would Hugo tell the truth about his cousin Samuel? Find out in the next exciting book!

* * *

Don't miss out!

Visit the website below and you can sign up to receive emails whenever Maxwell Hoffman publishes a new book. There's no charge and no obligation.

https://books2read.com/r/B-A-JVYOC-NDYCF

BOOKS 2 READ

Connecting independent readers to independent writers.

Did you love *Benny Dubious Playbook Scheme Trouble in Georgia Book 2: "Moshie's" Fall*? Then you should read *Benny Dubious Playbook Scheme Trouble in Georgia Book 1 The Moshie Affair*[1] by Ham Light!

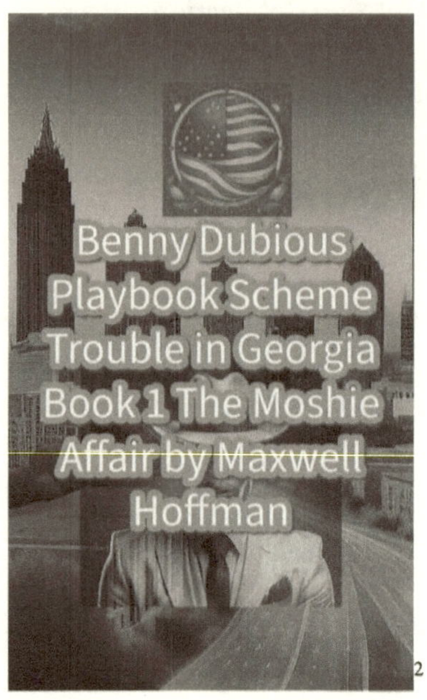

[2]

Join Benny Dubious in his latest capper as he descendants upon Atlanta, Georgia in the exciting election interference scandal! Benny has been hired by Samuel Roth of the Red, White and Secure to try to find out if his opponent - Ms. Nia Hope Carver has any scandals. He has asked Benny to have Hugo Roth to show him the trade of the game. However, Hugo soon makes up the name "Moshie Scheinman" at an event Nia is hosting with her father - Senator Amos Carver III approving of his presence.Hugo is soon torn between a moral objection and the duties of his cousin Samuel to distract Ms. Nia with his new persona!

---

1. https://books2read.com/u/booANZ

2. https://books2read.com/u/booANZ

About the Author

I graduated from California State University with a BA in History. I am fond of historical fiction, science fiction, fantasy, and horror.

Read more at https://www.instagram.com/vader7800/.

About the Publisher

I graduated from California State University of Northridge with a BA in History. I am fond of fantasy, science fiction, historical fiction and horror.

Read more at https://www.instagram.com/vader7800/.